The Berenstain Bears
and the
WEEK AT GRANDMA'S

When mama and papa bears
go away,
Cubs visit their grandparents
for their first long stay.

A FIRST TIME BOOK®

The Berenstain Bears

and the WEEK AT

Stan & Jan Berenstain

Random House 🏠 New York

Copyright © 1986 by Berenstains, Inc. All rights reserved under International and Pan-American Copyright Conventions. Published in the United States by Random House, Inc., New York, and simultaneously in Canada by Random House of Canada Limited, Toronto.

Library of Congress Cataloging-in-Publication Data: Berenstain, Stan. The Berenstain bears and the week at grandma's. (A First time book) SUMMARY: When Brother and Sister Bear get left with their grandparents for a whole week, they have a better time than they expected. [1. Bears—Fiction. 2. Grandparents—Fiction] I. Berenstain, Jan. II. Title. PZ7.B4483 Bernd 1986 [E] 85-25743 ISBN: 0-394-87335-1 (trade); 0-394-97335-6 (lib. bdg.)

Manufactured in the United States of America

JP/

39 40

GRANDMA'S

Once in a while the Bear family, who lived in the big tree house down a sunny dirt road deep in Bear Country, got out the family snapshots and looked at them.

"What are these?" asked Sister Bear, picking up a book of photos. "I don't think I've ever seen these before."

PHOTOS

There were pictures of bears playing tennis, canoeing, dancing, and having all sorts of fun. The bears looked like Mama and Papa, only they were younger and thinner.

"They're pictures of Papa and me on our honeymoon," said Mama with a smile.

"At Grizzly Mountain Lodge," said Papa. "We had a wonderful time!"

"What's a honeymoon?" asked Brother.

"A honeymoon is a special trip couples take when they get married," explained Mama. "Getting married is a very special happening, and celebrating it with a trip is an old custom."

"As a matter of fact," said Papa, "we've decided to go on a *second* honeymoon. We're going back to the same place and play tennis, go canoeing, and have fun!"

"It'll be lovely," said Mama.

PHOTOS

"A second honeymoon sounds like a pretty good idea to me," said Brother.

"Me, too," said Sister. They scooted out of the room and were back in a jiffy with their vacation things.

"Oh, you won't be coming," said Papa. "Honeymoons, even second honeymoons, are just for grownups, not for cubs."

"But . . . but what's going to happen to us?" asked Sister.

"It just so happens," said Mama, "that Gran has been after me to let you spend a week with her and Gramps. And this will be the perfect opportunity."

"A whole week?" said Brother.

"But we've never stayed with anybody that long!" said Sister.

"Well," said Papa, taking a few practice swings with his tennis racket, "there's got to be a first time for everything."

"What will we do for a whole week?" asked the cubs. "Where will we sleep? What will we eat?"

"Goodness!" said Mama. "Such a fuss about a simple thing like spending a week at Grandma's."

It didn't seem like a simple thing to the cubs. They loved Gramps and Gran very much, but ... well, they just weren't Mama and Papa.

Besides, Gramps and Gran were sort of ... *old.*

"What are you taking with you?" Sister asked Brother when it was time to pack. "I'm taking two books, my jacks, and my teddy, of course."

"These," he said, holding up some books and his best yo-yo.

Papa put their suitcases in the car trunk last so that when they got to Gran's, unloading was as easy as one-two-three.

Then, after lots of big bear hugs and kisses, the happy second honeymooners were on their way.

"It certainly is good to see young folks having fun," said Gran as she waved good-bye.

"*We're* the young folks," muttered the cubs. "*We're* the ones who are supposed to have fun."

"I'm sure you're hungry after your ride," said Gran when they went in. "How about some of my special honey nut cookies and milk?"

"No thanks, Gran," said Sister. "I'm not hungry right now."

"Hey, these are really good," said Brother.

Sister sneaked a taste. They *were* good, but... well, they just weren't Mama's.

"Now let's get you up to your room so you can get settled," said Gramps.

The cubs reached for their bags, but before you could say "Grizzly Gramps," they were gathered up, bags and all, and carried up the steep stairs. Gramps certainly was strong for someone so . . . *old*.

The room at the top of the stairs
was very nice—very nice, indeed,
but . . . well, it just wasn't home.

"Gramps," said Sister, "where do you suppose Mama and Papa are right now?"

"Well," said Gramps, "I reckon they're still on the road, just pulling into sight of Grizzly Mountain Lodge."

After they unpacked their things, Gramps thought the cubs might like to explore around the house.

While it wasn't home, it *was* an interesting house. There was the attic crowded with all *sorts* of interesting things . . .

Gran's kitchen with its yummy tastes and smells . . .

and Gramps' den. Gramps knew
how to build a ship in a
bottle. When the cubs asked
him how it was done, he just
smiled.

"What do you suppose Mama and Papa are doing now?" they asked then.

"I reckon they've gotten into their tennis clothes and are swatting the ball back and forth," he said.

Over the next few days Brother and Sister found lots to do. They helped Gran feed her bird friends— more kinds than they had ever seen in one place. And Gran knew all their names.

They helped Gramps cut and smooth twigs for a new ship in a bottle. It turned out that he built them *outside* the bottle and then slid them in. It was pretty tricky.

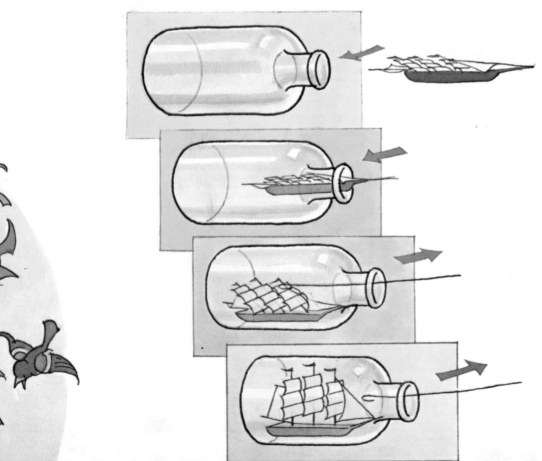

They went fishing in a special place Gramps knew about.

"Well," said Gramps as they returned with a fine catch, "I reckon that your mama and papa are out canoeing right now."

"I certainly hope they're having fun!" said Sister. "Because we sure are!"

"Hmm. Better get these chairs in,"
said Gramps after a fine fish fry.
"It's going to rain tomorrow."
    "How do you know?" asked Brother.
    "I can feel it in my bones,"
answered Gramps.

It turned out Gramps was right.

"Good," said Brother. "We'll be able to relax a little." Sister got out her jacks and he started to play with his yo-yo.

"Used to be pretty good with one of those myself," said Gramps.

Was he ever! Not only could Gramps make the yo-yo sleep and walk-the-dog, he could even do baby-in-the-cradle and round-the-world!

That evening, after a refreshing nap, they all went to Gramps and Gran's regular Friday night square dance.

Gramps and Gran didn't just watch. They do-si-doed with the best of them. They even won a prize—for Friskiest Couple.

"Goodness!" said Sister in the
morning. "This week really flew by!"

"And we learned so much," added
Brother, practicing baby-in-the-cradle.

"Gramps and Gran, how come you know so
much?" asked Sister. "So many things!
Why, you can even feel the weather in
your bones!"

"That's one of the good things about being an older person," said Gramps, smiling. "You learn something every day. So that by the time you're old enough to be a grandparent, you know quite a lot."

"Gee," said Sister, "I guess you and Gran are so old you must know *everything*!"

"Oh, no," said Gramps, laughing. "You never stop learning. Why, just this week we learned something very special. We learned how absolutely wonderful it is to be grandparents and have lovely grandcubs."

Then Gramps and Gran swept their grandcubs up in a big hug.

The next thing they knew, a familiar *beep! beep!* was heard. It was Papa tooting the horn. He and Mama were back from their second honeymoon and it was time for the cubs to go home.

After saying good-byes and thank-yous, the Bear family piled into the car and headed home. No sooner were they on their way than Brother and Sister were bubbling over with the fun and excitement of their week at Grandma's.

"Well," said Papa, "sounds like you had a pretty good time."

"Oh, we *did*!" said Sister. "Papa, sometime you might want to go on a *third* honeymoon. Then we could spend another week at Grandma's."

"A *third* honeymoon?" said Papa. "I don't think anyone's ever gone on a *third* honeymoon."

"Well," said Sister, "there has to be a first time for everything!"